FERGUS BARNABY

LIBRARIES NI
WITHDRAWN FROM STOCK

DAVID BARROW

D0682373

Fergus Barnaby lived on the first floor with Mum and Dad.

Today was a very exciting day because...

TEA
CITY
BEACH

...Fergus Barnaby was
going on holiday.

Mum and Dad were busy
fussing about getting packed.

"Ready yet, Fergus?" said Dad.
"Don't forget anything!"

"I've packed my suitcase," puffed
Fergus, "and – oh, no...

My bucket and spade!
I lent them to Fred
when we were
building a fort."

Fergus Barnaby
climbed up to the
second floor
where Fred lived.

"Hello, Fergus Barnaby."

"Hello, Fred. I'm going on holiday. Can I have my bucket and spade?"

"Of course, here you go. Send me a photo of your best castle."

27.

Fergus Barnaby

climbed all

the way

down from

the second floor

where Fred lived...

...to the

first floor

where he lived

with Mum and Dad.

He packed his bucket and spade.

"What else have you forgotten?" said Dad. He was starting to load up the car.

"Oh, no," said Fergus Barnaby. "My swimming goggles! I lent them to Emily Rose."

He climbed up to the third floor
where Emily Rose lived.

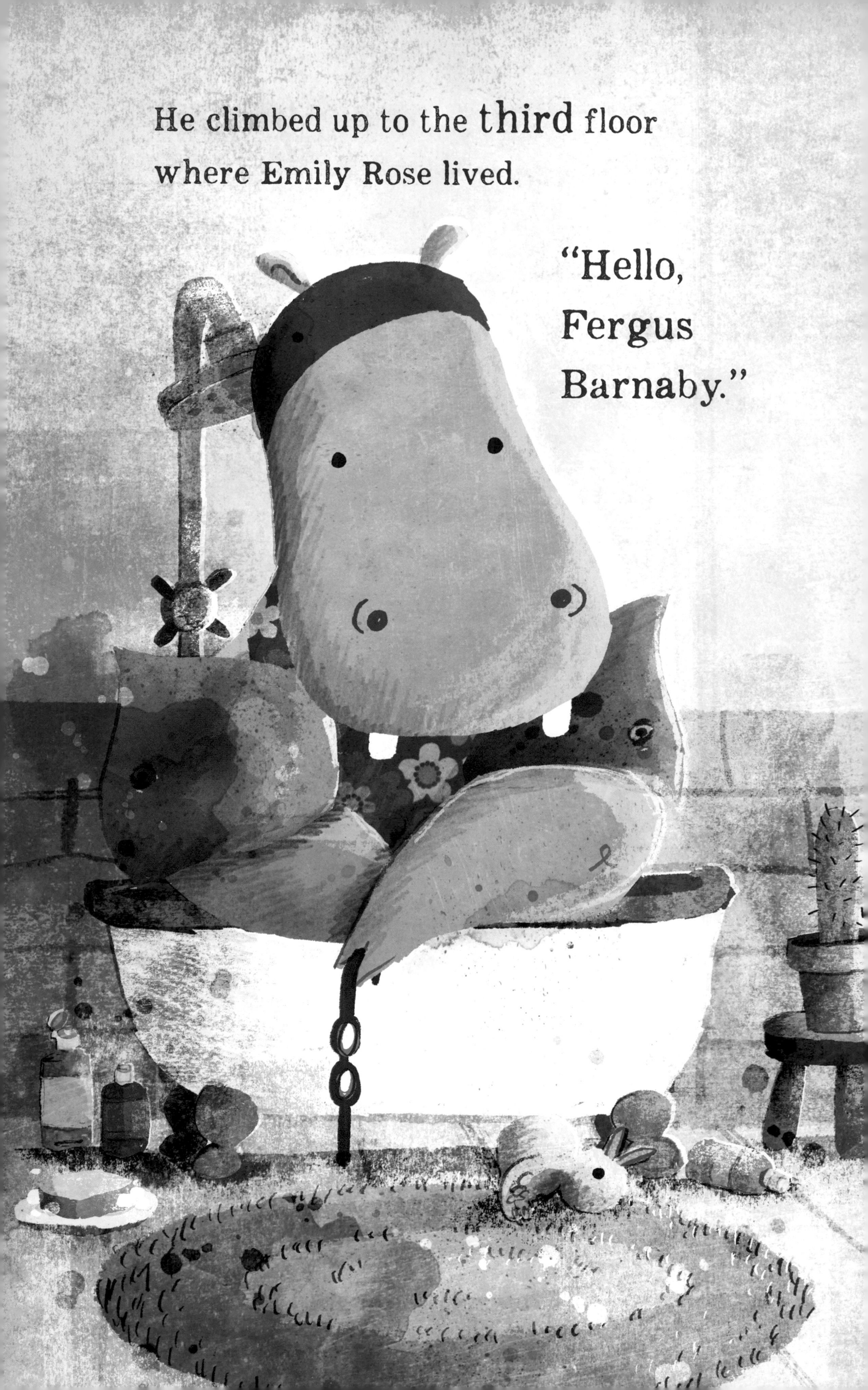

"Hello,
Fergus
Barnaby."

"Hello, Emily Rose. Can I have my swimming goggles? I'm going on holiday."

"Sure thing, here you go. Practice for when we go to swimming lessons together."

Fergus Barnaby climbed
all the way
down
down
from the third floor...
...to the first floor where
he lived with Mum and Dad.

...past the **second** floor where Fred lived who had borrowed his bucket and spade...

He packed his
swimming goggles.

"Is there anything else you've
forgotten?" said Dad checking the car.

"Oh, no," said Fergus Barnaby.
"My kite! I lent it to Teddy
when we were playing."

He climbed to the **fourth** floor
where Teddy lived.

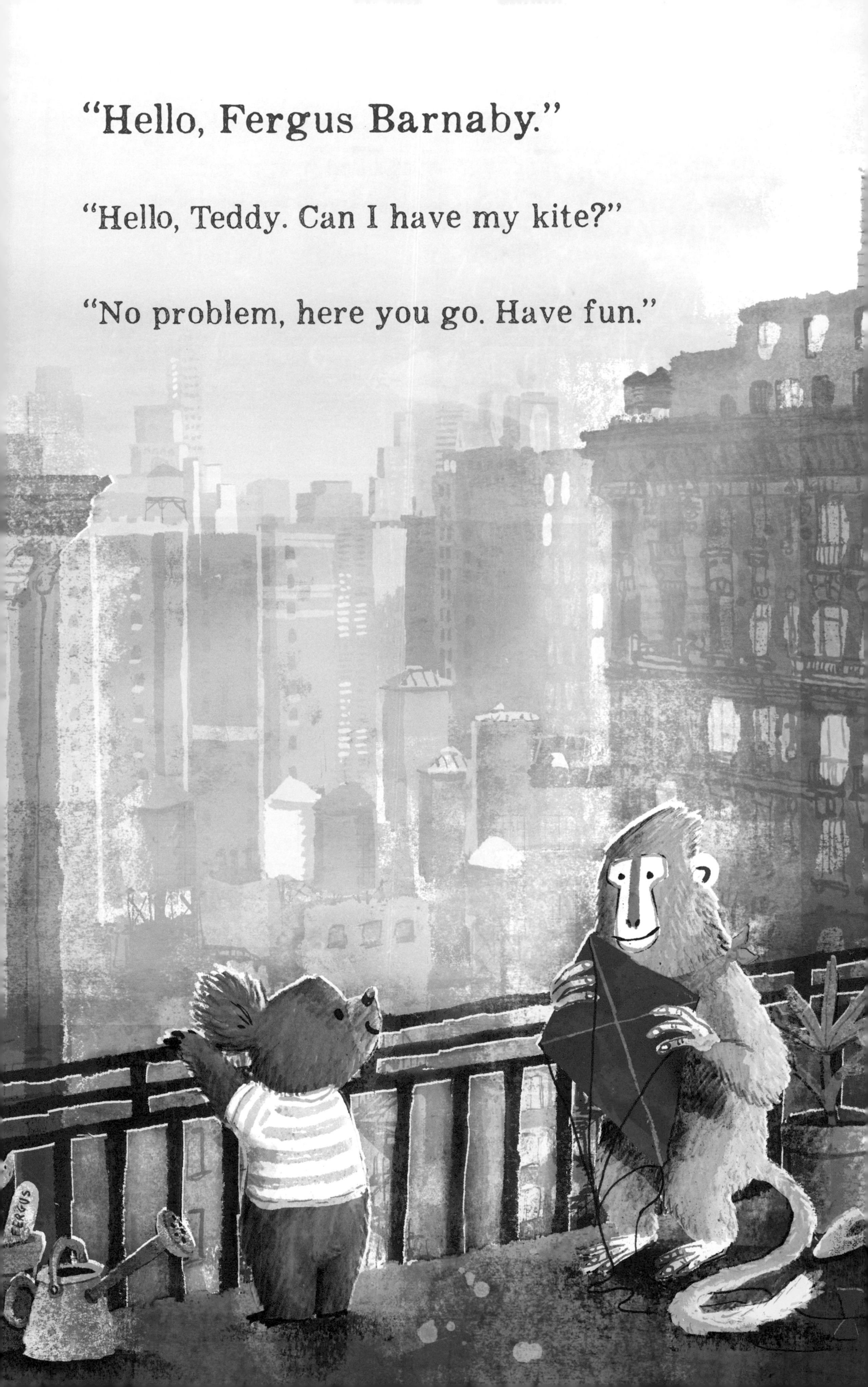

"Hello, Fergus Barnaby."

"Hello, Teddy. Can I have my kite?"

"No problem, here you go. Have fun."

Fergus Barnaby climbed all the way
down
down
down from the
fourth floor...
...past the second floor where
Fred lived who had borrowed his
bucket and spade...

...past the third floor where
Emily Rose lived who had borrowed
his swimming goggles...

...to the first floor where he
lived with Mum and Dad.

Fergus Barnaby packed his kite.
"Are you ready now?" said Dad.

"Oh, YES," said Fergus Barnaby.
"I think I am!"

CITY LIMITS 2
SEASIDE 42

And so they set
off on holiday.

"OH, NO!" said
Fergus Barnaby...

"Fergus Barnaby!" said Dad.

"You went up to the fourth floor to get your kite from Teddy.

You went up to the third floor to get your swimming goggles from Emily Rose.

You went up to the second floor to get your bucket and spade from Fred.

You packed your suitcase on the
first floor where we live.

What could you possibly
have forgotten?"

"WE'VE FORGOTTEN MUM!"

For the real Teddy

**With infinite thanks to Jenny & Emma
for their unwavering ingenuity**

HODDER CHILDREN'S BOOKS
First published in Great Britain in 2017 by Hodder Children's Books

Copyright © Dave Barrow, 2017

The moral rights of the author have been asserted.
All rights reserved

A CIP catalogue record for this book is available from the British Library.

ISBN: 9781 444 92904 1

10 9 8 7 6 5 4 3 2 1

Printed and bound in China

MIX
Paper from responsible sources
FSC® C104740

Hodder Children's Books, an imprint of Hachette Children's Group, part of Hodder and Stoughton,
Carmelite House, 50 Victoria Embankment, London, EC4Y 0DZ

An Hachette UK Company
www.hachette.co.uk
www.hachettechildrens.co.uk